T0082683

Faith
UnBrOkEn

ARTHUR DUNLAP JR.

WESTBOW
PRESS®
A DIVISION OF THOMAS NELSON
& ZONDERVAN

WestBow Press books may be ordered through booksellers or by contacting:

WestBow Press
A Division of Thomas Nelson & Zondervan
1663 Liberty Drive
Bloomington, IN 47403
www.westbowpress.com
1 (866) 928-1240

ISBN: 978-1-9736-1854-6 (sc)
ISBN: 978-1-9736-1855-3 (e)

Library of Congress Control Number: 2018901473

Print information available on the last page.

WestBow Press rev. date: 02/15/2018

Defining Faith

The biblical definition of faith is trusting in something you cannot prove. Faith is confidence and the substance of things we hope for as well as the assurance about what we do not see. It is also our handle on what we cannot see. Trust in God, our faith in Him, is the firm foundation under everything that makes life worth living.

Defining Unbroken

An adjective meaning not broken, fractured, damaged, or impaired. Is intact or whole.

Faith

God has provided us with faith,

Which is something we cannot see,

To find out if we really have trust

In him and if we truly believe

That if light fell to pierce through

The clouds on a rainy day.

If we have faith, for it is then

That he will lead the way.

We always walk in darkness,

Not blind but still cannot see.

Having faith in God is a blessing,

No matter how bad things may be.

Having faith the size of a

Grain of mustard seed

Assures us that God will be there

For us in times of need.

Let us hold steadfast to God's

guiding light.

All we need to do is walk by faith

And not by sight.

Amen.

Faith
UnBrOkEn

Some people may look at my adult life, and come to the conclusion that my whole life has been great. To shine a light on that assumption, I will take you on a little journey.

My name is Oscar Williams, and I was raised by a single parent, my mother, Maggie Williams. One would think life was rough for me as an only child, but this was not true. My mother told me that my father (whom I never met) died in the war in Iraq when I was a baby, not saying much more about him. We lived in a rough part of Detroit with gangs, drugs, and killings. She would always tell me that she would do whatever she could to protect me from those surroundings.

Unfortunately, my mother passed away from cancer when I was ten years old. My mother's sister and only living relative, Bethe Brown, took me in to raise me. My aunt was single and had no children. There were rumors that she could not have children. She lived in a nice part of Detroit in a well-to-do neighborhood, which was a big change from where I used to live.

After my mother's death, I was bitter as well as rebellious. Looking back, I realize my aunt did all she could to make my life comfortable. Being a hurt child, I did not realize that at the time.

My aunt's belief in God was strong. She prayed a lot and went to church regularly. She always told me that if I believed and trusted in God, for every bad thing that happens, God would replace it with something good. She would tell me this over and over again. As a child, I was irritated by those words, not knowing that eventually they would become my words. She would also tell me that with God in my life, I could overcome anything.

In the beginning, school was terrible for me. I had a bad attitude, to say the least. I was disobedient, but through it all my aunt hung in there with me. She would tell me time and time again that she was not giving up on me. School counselors and our family doctor felt that I needed to be on medication for

ADHD, but she refused their recommendations. She was not hard on me, but she was firm. She let me know that if I did not do well in school, and if my attitude did not get better, there would be no perks coming my way from her.

My aunt enrolled me in piano lessons, which I hated. It was not until I went out for the church basketball team that my life took a turn for the better. The coach of the church basketball team, Ben Jackson, took a special interest in me. Personally, I thought he had eyes for my aunt. "Coach Jack" taught me to use my anger in a positive way, which I did, and I became the star—not only of the church team but also the church basketball league.

I graduated from high school at the top of my class. After playing basketball in high school, I received a scholarship to college, with the full support of my aunt. I graduated from college and landed a job at one of the top finance firms in the country. I knew how blessed I was, and I thanked God every day for how my life had evolved. I went to church regularly, prayed often, and constantly let people know how blessed I was.

I eventually met the love of my life, Sherri Dunn. We got married and had a son named Oscar Jr., which completed my world. I could not have asked for a better life.

My aunt became sick and was bedridden. I was crushed because I loved my aunt so much, and to see her sick hurt me to the core. I never prayed so much and so hard in my life. She kept telling me how God works and we have to trust, believe, and accept his decisions. She said that was the foundation of faith. Even though I did not want to see my aunt in pain or even die, when she finally passed away to be with God, I was totally at peace with it. Her passing brought me even closer to God.

I continued to realize how blessed I was with a beautiful wife and son. My life was great. I had a lovely home, nice vehicles, and a large income because I was the top finance officer in the firm. Also, I was very active in church. My life was great—thanks to God.

From time to time, my aunt used to tell me our faith in God may someday be tested. When she passed away, I felt I had lost my rock, but my faith in God let me know that he, God, was my rock.

Every Wednesday night, my family and I went to church for Bible study. We always went to church together, but one day I had to work late, so my wife and son were to meet me there. I got to church a little late to find out that my wife and son were not there. I wasn't worried; still, I called her on her cell phone, which went straight to her voicemail. I said a prayer and continued to participate in Bible study.

Moments later, my cell phone rang. What I heard, I definitely was not ready for. The caller introduced himself as a police officer. After hearing that, I went totally numb, I went deaf, and I got a lump in my throat. It seemed as if the whole world had stopped. This all happened before the officer said anything else. After he introduced himself, I remember hearing him ask me if I was Oscar Williams. Then he said, "Sir, are you there?"

Not knowing everything he had already said, I responded, "Yes, this is Oscar Williams." He said that my wife and son were in an accident, and I should come to University Hospital right away. When I heard that, I dropped my cell phone and collapsed to the floor.

Not knowing what I had heard, church members gathered around me and began to pray. I let it be known that I needed to go to the hospital. Seeing how upset I was, the pastor drove me to the hospital. After arriving, I learned that my wife and son were dead. An officer informed me the road my family was traveling on collapsed, and my wife's car fell forty feet into a hole, killing them both instantly. According to the officer, the road caved in due to heavy rain we had gotten days earlier. Tears and pain have accompanied me from that moment on.

After my pastor dropped me off at my house, I went into a deep depression. I got on my knees and tried to pray, but for some odd reason, I could not pray. I cried out to God and told him I needed him. I could hear my aunt's voice telling me to keep the faith. She used to tell me that some people who had faith in God when things were going well seemed to abandon their faith when things went bad because they felt God was not there for them in their time of need. My aunt used to say that she could not understand why people would lose their faith in God at a time when they needed him the most.

The more I tried to pray, the more my body ached, and the more I cried. I could not eat or sleep, nor could I pray. I was in a place and state of mind that was unexplainable. All I could do was lie on my couch in a fetal position and cry. Nothing on this earth meant anything to me, including myself. Here I was in this world, and all of the people I had ever loved were gone.

My aunt used to tell me, "When all is lost, you can always turn to God." She said things will happen in this life that we may not understand, but we have to continue to believe in God, have faith in him, and let his will be done.

I was isolated on my couch—not eating, not sleeping, not communicating with others, not taking care of my personal hygiene, and not going to work. Friends, in-laws, coworkers, and church members reached out to me, but I did not respond to the doorbell, nor did I answer my phone. I was in such a dark place that I could not arrange the funeral for my wife and son, nor did I want to attend. I am thankful and indebted to my in-laws for taking care of the funeral arrangements. Some people judged me even though I attended the wake and funeral without anyone's knowledge. Their judgement meant nothing to me.

Because I was drowning in my sorrow, no bills were getting paid. I was not working, so my home phone, cell phone, electricity, and water were shut off, and all my vehicles were repossessed. My house was foreclosed on. Those material things meant nothing to me. All I wanted was my family back. I missed them so much.

All the things that had happened to me were grounds for me to question God and my faith, but for some reason I could not. Not once did I say God, "Why me?" It was hard to keep faith in God. But I had no one else but him, so I had to hold on to his unchanging hand. If I could only pray, I believed some of my hurt would go away.

I then became homeless, sleeping on bus stop benches, on park benches, and under overpasses. That was my life. Though I once ate at fine restaurants, I now ate from garbage cans and dumpsters. I really did not care about myself and the shape I was in. All I wanted was to be left alone.

While I was looking for food in a dumpster one day, a strange thing happened. I came across a book titled *Faith*. When I saw the book, there was this light around it, as if it were glowing. Let me remind you that this book was in a dumpster full of trash and liquids. It was nighttime, and the only light was from the moon. The book was laying there among the rubbish with no stains or dirt on it. It was as if it was placed there just for me.

I removed the book from the dumpster and placed it inside my shirt next to my heart, protecting it as if it was a treasure. I walked to a nearby park and sat on a bench illuminated by a streetlight. As I began to read the book called *Faith*, my whole body and mind-set began to change. The pain that accompanied my body had gone. This weight that burdened my body seemed to have been lifted. Life seemed to matter again. Even the sorrow I had was gone.

Passages in this book helped me to turn my life around. Not only was I feeling better, but I could also pray again. This book pointed out to me that when we have faith in God, he will provide us with everything we need to overcome whatever problems we encounter here on earth. He gives us the ability to heal not only others but ourselves as well. He has instilled in us to achieve whatever goals we desire, whether mentally or physically. I felt the reason I could not pray was because God wanted me to get through my problems with what he had already blessed me with. Sometimes God blesses us way before we need the blessing.

With the pain, tears, sorrow, and grief lifted off of my shoulders, I realized I had to get my act together.

Sometimes the troubles we have, we bring on ourselves. We have to accept the things we cannot control and move on. I knew that for me to be a good servant of God, I had to get my life back in order. How could I serve God when I was not serving myself?

Reading the book *Faith* let me know that God's plan for us may be a different plan than we have for ourselves. A lot of things I read in the book sounded a lot like what my aunt used to tell me. If I did not know better, I would have thought that she wrote this book. We may not know what God's plan is for us. All we have to do is trust in him and follow his lead, and we will accomplish what he has in store for us.

I learned a lot about life from this book. I learned things about death, which had sent my life into a tailspin. God chose to make death a part of our lives and a part of this world. Who are we to challenge God's work? I understand now that those who died that I loved died for a reason. Their death was not designed to hurt me or destroy my life. Their deaths were in some way there to strengthen me. God had put people in my life for me to love, and he chose to call them home. Now that I was able to pray again, I made sure to thank God for putting them in my life and for giving me the chance to have loved them.

Now that my head was in a better place, it was time for me to get my life back in order. The situation I was in was all on me, so it was up to me to turn things around. I knew God had something in store for me, and it was up to me to prepare myself for his blessing.

In the past, God had blessed me with a wonderful life, a loving wife and son, a nice home, a good job, and lots of nice material things. My life was not perfect then, but I was happy and thankful for how my life was. It was obvious God had something different in store for me.

There was a passage in *Faith* that made me aware of blessings. It stated God blesses us so we can pass blessings on to others. It was time for me to find a way to pass blessings on to others, which I had not done in the past.

Now that my mind was thinking straight, I knew I had to get myself together. Even though I had college degrees, I did not want to be in the corporate workforce. I applied for a job at a local hospital. The only position available was janitorial. I was offered the job, which I accepted. I did not put my college degrees on the application because I did not want to be overqualified for the job.

It seemed my life had changed a lot in a short period of time. I felt that now I was embarking on a new journey for God. I was grateful for all God had done for me. Even through my trials and turmoil, God continued to bless and watch over me. When I slept outside on benches, he was there protecting me from all harm. It was not until I reflected on the past that I realized just how blessed I was.

My job at the hospital was on the night shift, five days a week. It was a far cry from the corporate job I once had, as well as the income, but I was okay with that. My job was to clean bathrooms and mop floors on two different wards, children and adults. Now that my job situation was together, my living status also changed, which was a big change from my previous living conditions.

Working in a hospital was a challenge. Because of the patients and their families dealing with various illnesses, diseases, and sometimes death, I heard cries and moans on a regular basis. I found myself praying for patients all the time. At first, I would pray for patients when I was by myself in the storage room, but I was driven to lay hands on patients and pray for them in their rooms. I know that putting my hands on patients was not proper, but that was what I felt I should do.

Once I laid hands on patients, I often noticed that after praying for them, they got much better. Some of the patients, who had been hospitalized for months, were released to go home, feeling much better shortly after I touched them. Doctors and family members were baffled by the sudden turnaround of the patients.

The more patients I prayed for, the more patients got better. No one was aware that I was praying for these patients who were recovering. I would go into patients' rooms while they slept, lay a hand on their forehead, pray for them, and quickly leave. In some cases when I returned to work, patients had already been released and sent home doing much better.

There was one little boy I took a liking to. I do not know if he reminded me of my son, but out of all the patients I prayed for, he was one of my favorites. His recovery was not as quick as some of the other patients I prayed for. The doctors had said that the boy's illness was not curable, and he had a short time to live. For a parent to hear that news, it has to be heartbreaking.

One night when I was leaving his room, he awakened and said, "Hello." I continued to walk out of the room, not looking back or saying anything. I knew this was awkward, but God works in strange ways. I was comfortable laying hands on patients and praying for them, but I was not comfortable speaking to them.

Rumors were spreading throughout the hospital about miracles that were happening on the two wards I worked on. Doctors were confused, and family members of the patients were puzzled but overjoyed with the recovery of their loved ones. God was answering not only my prayers but the prayers of others as well.

I was feeling good about my life. *Faith* had helped turn my life completely around. In the past, I paid my tithes and offerings to church regularly, but there was more that God wanted me to do. Now I was put in the position to help others. God had blessed me to lay hands on others, and through his blessing, I was able to bring some healing to those who were going through health problems. Not in my wildest dreams did I think that God would use me in this way.

The young boy patient eventually got much better and went home fully recovered. Seeing him recover warmed my heart to the highest degree. I could not have been prouder for him.

As we all know, in life where there is good there is bad. While there was joy on the wards where I worked, there was trouble also. I was not aware of the rumors going around the hospital that someone was going into patients' rooms and stealing personal items like cell phones, money, and other items. I stayed to myself and never communicated with other hospital employees other than saying hello or good morning.

I began to notice police officers on patients' floors, but I did not think much of it. Seeing them in and around the emergency room and on wards was common. I never was concerned about their presence.

Now events were beginning to get really interesting. I was called to my supervisor's office to be questioned. In my supervisor's office were two detectives who were questioning employees concerning the recent robberies in the hospital. According to the detectives, because I frequented the floors where robberies had happened and because my job description was to mop floors and clean restrooms in patients' rooms, I had to be questioned. It was just routine questioning, nothing more, according to the detectives. I was comfortable answering their questions.

They asked me if I had ever taken anything from patients' rooms intentionally or unintentionally, and

I answered no to both questions. They also asked me if I noticed anyone going in and out of patients' rooms who did not seem to belong in them. Once again, I said no. They asked me if I was sure about taking something out of patients' rooms accidentally. I said no. They asked me if I would answer more questions at a later time if needed, to which I said yes. I was given the okay to leave.

Two weeks later, I was asked to come to the police station for questioning. I thought that was odd, but I agreed to do it. The first question I was asked was, "Did you take anything from patients' rooms?" I responded no. They asked me my age, about my relationships past and present, any addictions, my lifestyle, my work habits, my family and friends, and if I have any enemies. Because of the nature of the questions, I asked the detectives if I was a suspect, and they informed me that everyone who worked at the hospital was a suspect. After three hours of questioning, I was allowed to leave.

The next day at work my supervisor informed me that my work requirements had changed. I would no longer be entering patients' rooms to clean or mop. I was limited to cleaning hallways and hallway restrooms only. My supervisor explained to me that this was temporary until the investigation about the robberies was finished.

Two weeks passed since the change at work. Strangely enough, the robberies stopped, and the mystery healing of patients stopped as well. I was resting at my apartment when there was a knock at my door. I was shocked to see it was the detectives from the police station who were there to inform me that I was being arrested for the robberies at the hospital. I was handcuffed and taken to the police station. I was read my rights and given the right to an attorney. They asked if I would like to talk to them and if so, if I would like to have an attorney present. I said that I was okay answering their questions without a lawyer present.

Their questions to me were a lot more intense than the questions they asked before. The interrogation went on for hours, and then I was led off to jail. Because of my faith in God, I knew that I would eventually be cleared of all charges and set free.

While I was in jail, the inmates called me Rev even though I was not a pastor. Life seemed as if it was not going my way, but I felt God was still with me and protecting me, as he had my entire life. I remembered what my aunt and *Faith* said—when life goes bad, that is the time you need God the most. My faith in God and my prayers became my strength and armor.

When I went before a judge, he asked me if I had a lawyer and I said no. He said if I could not afford a lawyer that the courts would appoint me a public defendant, which they did.

Two weeks after I was incarcerated, I was informed that I had a visitor. I was surprised because I never called or communicated with anyone concerning my situation, even though I was given the opportunity to make a phone call. When I met my visitor, it was like looking at an angel from heaven. She was the prettiest female that I had ever seen since seeing my wife for the first time.

I had a puzzled look on my face. I thought that she was visiting me by mistake. She said she was a lawyer, and she was here to represent me in my case. I thanked her for taking my case and said how pleased I was with the judge for appointing her as my lawyer. She told me that she was not appointed by the courts to represent me, and neither was she a public defender. I let her know that I did not have the funds to hire an attorney. She said that she would represent me at no cost (a.k.a., pro bono). I was so delighted.

I asked her why she would take me on as a client for free, and her response nearly brought me to tears. Plus, it let me know just how God works and how he answers prayers. She said her son was gravely ill and in the hospital and was given only a short time to live. She said that even though she did not go to church and never prayed, she hoped that the doctors were wrong in their diagnosis of her son. She said that when she visited him, she noticed he was improving, and so did the doctors. She said the doctors said he was improving to the point where he was ready to be released. She said only God could have blessed her and her son with this miracle.

She said after her son was released from the hospital with a clean bill of health, while driving him home, all she could do was cry tears of joy and thank God in a silent prayer. She said a few weeks after taking her son home from the hospital, they were watching television together, and the local news came on reporting that they had arrested a suspect in the hospital robberies. She said the news she was watching showed a picture of me as the suspect. It was at that moment that when her son said he knew me. She said she was shocked to hear him say that, so she asked him how he knew me. He said I was the friend who would come into his room at night, lay a hand on his forehead, and pray for him. He said I was the reason he had gotten better. She said she asked him why he did not mention to her that someone was coming into his room and praying for him. He said he did not know if she would have believed him because he felt that I was someone sent by God to help heal him from his illness. She told him that no matter what the situation was, he could always talk to her about anything.

She asked him if he was sure that the man they were showing on television was the same man who entered his room several times. He answered yes. Her son also told her that at first, he thought he was dreaming about me coming into his room, and that was the reason he did not mention it to her.

She told me that her name was Angela Miles and that her son's name was Tye Miles, named after his father. I found out later that he was a soldier who was killed fighting in the Afghanistan war two years earlier.

She said she would look into my case, and try to get me a bond hearing. She said she could not wait to get home to tell her son that she had taken my case, and I was her client. She said she knew her son would be delighted. I could not wait to get back to my cell and thank God for sending her to represent me. Just like the words in *Faith* said, sometimes the worst things that happens in one's life can turn out to be the best thing in one's life—if you have faith in God. All you have to do is believe in him.

It may sound strange to some people, but I was comfortable being incarcerated because for one, I was innocent, and I had faith in God to see me through this. Good or bad, things happen for a reason. We may not understand why things happen, but just like *Faith* said, some things are not meant to be understood.

While I was in jail, I decided to spread the word of God. I would talk about faith and believing and trusting in him. I told other inmates to try to make the best of their situation, no matter how bad it may seem. I told them to pray, keep the faith, and keep looking to God because one day this too shall pass.

While in jail, I never thought about time. I was more focus on praying, reading, and exercising. One day I got a message that my lawyer was there to visit. She was there to inform me that she had arranged a bond hearing for me. I was pleased to hear it. I wanted to let her know how thankful I was for her help, but I wanted to point out that I did not want her to feel obligated to me because of my praying for her son and his healing. I let her know it was not me who healed her son. It was God who deserved all the credit. God just happened to use me to deliver his healing. She said God must have sent her to help me as well. I could only smile. I probably should be amazed at how God works, but I am not. Because after all, he is God.

Once my attorney told me about the bond hearing and the date, she gave me something that was really heart-warming. Her son had a picture for me, which brought tears to my eyes. It was a picture of a child placing his hand on the forehead of a man with the caption reading, "You prayed for me, and now I pray for you." How touching!

While I was incarcerated, I had time to reflect on my life and life in general. Even with my situation, I realized how blessed I was and how God had been by my side. Belief, prayer, and faith have been my companion. Once I prayed and turned things over to God, I was sure that life would be okay. I knew of my innocence, and God knew as well. What other people thought about me did not matter because I knew that with God's help, the truth would eventually come to the surface.

With my bond hearing coming up in one week, my attorney felt the chance of me getting bond was good. She was excited for me knowing I would soon be freed from jail. She noticed I was not showing any excitement about getting out on bond. I let her know that once this was behind me, I would rejoice. *Faith* said joy will come in the morning. I was waiting for the morning to come.

People have to learn how to take a bad situation and turn it into something positive. While in jail, I was blessed to meet some nice people, which resulted in a friendship between two other inmates and myself. We formed a gospel singing group that actually turned out to be pretty good (if I do say so myself).

One of the inmates was a man named Ken Frazier who was in jail because his brother used his identity and got speeding tickets in his name and never showed up in court or paid the tickets, which resulted in an arrest warrant. Ken eventually was arrested.

The other inmate was Liam Wilson, arrested for back child support, which was incorrect because it was later revealed that he had no children. Eventually both men were released, and their charges were dropped. I was in charge of the jail's library, which allowed us to practice singing in one of the reading rooms, which was great.

Finally, my bond hearing date came. It was good to get out of government-issued clothing and to wear civilian clothes for a change. My attorney was able to obtain a suit from my apartment for me. We appeared in court before a judge, and I was granted a bond until my next court appearance. My lawyer made it clear to me that the evidence against me was speculation at best. The prosecutor wanted some restrictions on my release, but the judge felt differently, thank God. I was freed on bond with no restrictions.

My attorney said that she viewed the state's evidence and was pretty sure she could get the charges against me dropped. I was not worried because I had prayed and put my situation in God's hand. Sometimes in life we have to go through hardships in order to get to better opportunities. It was a joy to be free. It was a joy to see my attorney's son for the first time since he was released from the hospital. I was able to thank him personally for the card he sent me, which was very uplifting. He also thanked me for the prayers that I prayed for him during his stay in the hospital.

To show my appreciation to my lawyer and her son, I nervously invited them out for dinner. I was nervous because I had not been on a date with a woman since the passing of my wife. To my delight, she accepted my dinner offer.

Freedom is something some people take for granted. Being confined made me appreciate not only my freedom but life in general. The air smelled better. Food tasted better. Things around me looked better. That is why I thank God every day for all of the blessings he has given me.

With my trial coming up, I met with my lawyer to discuss my case. I was curious to know what evidence the state had against me. During our meeting, my lawyer said that the state's case against me was weak.

They had no evidence tying me to the robberies. I knew that God had everything worked out for me. Feeling that way is a great feeling—a feeling like no other.

I told my lawyer if they looked at the hospital's surveillance cameras, they would see I was not the one stealing from patients' rooms. She said at this hospital there were no cameras on wards or in patients' rooms because of patients' privacy. The hospital where I worked only had cameras at the entrances, parking areas, and parking garage elevators.

She said even though she did not pray, go to church, or believe in God at first, once God healed her son, she now had faith in God, went to church, and even prayed daily. She admitted that at first, she did not know how to pray, but after she started reading the Bible, she learned how. She said God had let her know that we would beat the charges against me. Hearing her say those words gave me a good feeling.

With my trial only a week away, I received a call from my attorney telling me the charges against me had been dropped, and the police had arrested the person who was stealing out of patients' room. It turned out that the person they arrested was a female who was dressed in a hospital worker's uniform. Once I was arrested, the robberies on the wards where I worked had stopped, but before I was out of jail on bond, the robberies soon start happening again.

I was told the police used undercover officers to watch patients' rooms and were able to catch the thief. Once they thought they had the right person, they got a warrant to check the suspect's home and found items stolen from the hospital. Hearing this news was music to my ears. Not only was it good for me, but for the patients at the hospital.

With the twists, the turns, the ups, the downs, the good, and the bad that occurs in life, having faith in God helps me to stand strong like a tree in a storm. Not knowing which way the winds will blow, but knowing that God will be there for me at all times is mammoth.

Two years have passed, and there has been a lot of changes in my life. God called me to pastor. I went back to school to further my education in ministry. Ironically, I am now the pastor of the church that my aunt took me to as a child. Yes, I am the pastor of Christ Temple Church of God. Just to point out how God works, some of the members who talked negatively about me and turned their backs on me when I went through my ordeal joined with me to make Christ Temple a strong place to worship. Thanks goes to my aunt for putting me in a position where I ended up being a servant of God. God chose me as one of his shepherds to prepare his flock for eternal life with him, which I am honored to do.

My personal life changed as well. Surprisingly, Angela and I started dating shortly after my court situation was over. We are married now, and my two friends from jail, Ken and Liam, sang at our wedding. It was a grand event. I adopted her son, Tye. Angela became pregnant, and I could not have been happier. After the death of my wife and son, I never thought that I could love again, but God put Angela in my life and proved me wrong.

In my wildest dream, I would never have thought that my life would be at this point. Just like *Faith* said, God works in mysterious ways. Not only did this book help me in my life's journey, but it also taught me to appreciate God even more. Because of his greatness, during my daily prayers, I let him know just how much I love him.

I have to share the good news that my wife and I are expecting twins. When the doctor told us that we were having twins, I fainted. While I was semiconscious, I could hear a voice calling my name, telling me to wake up. As strange as this may seem, the voice telling me to wake up sounded like my first wife. When I regained consciousness and opened my eyes, there standing over me was my first wife, Sherri, and standing beside her was my son, Oscar Jr. It turned out, that during all of this time, I was dreaming. My aunt had passed away, but my first wife and son were still alive. What a blessing. God is good, and my faith in him is supreme. Unseen, unspoken, that is faith, let it be unbroken.

Amen.

Printed in the United States
By Bookmasters